R・・7

Knight Fight

Written by Lesley Sims

Illustrated by Lee Cosgrove

How this book works

The story of **Knight Fight** has been written for your child to read with your help. Encourage your child to read as much as they can, helping to sound out the words and explaining any meanings if they get stuck.

A sign is on the castle wall.

Jousting today— open to all!

There are puzzles after the story, and for these you may need to read the instructions to your child.

You can find out more about helping your child with this book, and with reading in general, on pages 30-31.

2

Knight Fight

Turn the page to start the story.

A sign is on
the castle wall.

Jousting
today—
open to
all!

The gold knight reads it
with a grin.

Jousting
today—
open to
all!

The gold knight thunders down the track.

He's like
a rhino
on attack.

His lance gets stuck.

His horse just stops.

The gold knight soars and belly-flops.

"Ow! Ow!" he moans.
"I ache. I hurt."

"My wrists are sore,
my toes are numb."

A solemn hush...
then he stands up.

The knights shake hands.
The people cheer.

The gold knight says,
"See you next year!"

Puzzle 1

Look at the pictures, read the sentences, then say whether they are true or false.

1.

There is a sign about a feast.

2.

The gold knight grins.

3.

The gold knight is hurt.

4.

The knights rub noses.

Puzzle 2

Choose the right word for each sentence.

1.

The silver knight | signs | | sighs | .

2.

The gold | knife | | knight | soars.

3.

"My wrists are sore sure ."

4.

"The shiver silver knight deserves the cup."

Puzzle 3

These pairs of words share a letter that you don't hear when you say the words. Can you find the 'silent' letter in each pair?

palm	half
wrist	wriggle
numb	thumb
knight	knee
rhino	rhyme

Answers to puzzles

Puzzle 1

1. False
2. True
3. True
4. False

Puzzle 2

1. The silver knight sighs.
2. The gold knight soars.
3. "My wrists are sore."
4. "The silver knight deserves the cup."

Puzzle 3

palm	half	l
wrist	wriggle	w
numb	thumb	b
knight	knee	k
rhino	rhyme	h

Guidance notes

Usborne Very First Reading is a series of books, specially developed for children who are learning to read. **Knight Fight** is the fourteenth book in the series, and by this stage your child should be able to read the story alone, with occasional help from you.

The story of **Knight Fight** introduces the "silent consonants" in combinations of letters such as:

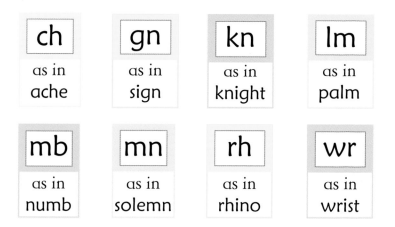

ch	**gn**	**kn**	**lm**
as in ache	as in sign	as in knight	as in palm

mb	**mn**	**rh**	**wr**
as in numb	as in solemn	as in rhino	as in wrist

These can be tricky to read, and even more to spell.

You'll find lots more information about the structure of the series, advice on helping your child with reading, extra practice activities and games on the Very First Reading website,* **www.usborne.com/veryfirstreading**

*US readers go to **www.veryfirstreading.com**

Some questions and answers

- **Why do I need to read with my child?**
  Sharing stories makes reading an enjoyable and fun activity for children. It also helps them to develop confidence and stamina. Even if you are not taking an active part in reading, your listening and support are very important.

- **When is a good time to read?**
  Choose a time when you are both relaxed, but not too tired, and there are no distractions. Only read for as long as your child wants to – you can always try again another day.

- **What if my child gets stuck?**
  Don't simply read the problem word yourself, but prompt your child and try to find the right answer together. Similarly, if your child makes a mistake, go back and look at the word together. Don't forget to give plenty of praise and encouragement.

- **We've finished, now what do we do?**
  It's a good idea to read the story several times to give your child more practice and more confidence. Then, when your child is ready, you can go on to the final book in the series, **Mr. Mystery.**

Edited by Jenny Tyler and Mairi Mackinnon
Designed by Russell Punter

First published in 2010 by Usborne Publishing Ltd., Usborne House,
83-85 Saffron Hill, London EC1N 8RT, England. www.usborne.com
Copyright © 2010 Usborne Publishing Ltd.

E VERY FIRST READING

...ifteen titles in the Usborne
...eading series, which has been
...ped to help children learn to read.

... about the structure of the series,
...w.veryfirstreading.com

2

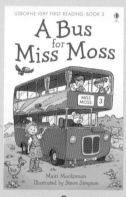

3

5

6

USBORN

Th**ere** are

Very **First R**

specially develop

To find out more

g**o** to ww

USBORNE VERY FIRST READI**NG: BOOK 1**

Pirate Pat

Mairi Mackin
Illustrated by Mike and Carl Gordon

1

USBORNE VERY FIRST READI**NG: BOOK 4**

Dog
Dia**ry**

Mairi Mackin
Illustrated by

4

USBORNE VERY FIRST READING

There are fifteen titles in the **Usborne Very First Reading** series, which has been specially developed to help children learn to read.

To find out more about the structure of the series, go to **www.veryfirstreading.com**

USBORNE VERY FIRST READING: BOOK 1
Pirate Pat
Mairi Mackinnon
Illustrated by Mike and Carl Gordon
1

USBORNE VERY FIRST READING: BOOK 2
The Dressing-Up Box
Mairi Mackinnon
Illustrated by Kate Sheppard
2

USBORNE VERY FIRST READING: BOOK 3
A Bus for Miss Moss
Mairi Mackinnon
Illustrated by Steve Simpson
3

USBORNE VERY FIRST READING: BOOK 4
Dog Diary
Mairi Mackinnon
Illustrated by Fred Blunt
4

USBORNE VERY FIRST READING: BOOK 5
Grizzly Bear Rock
Lesley Sims
Illustrated by Andrew Rowland
5

USBORNE VERY FIRST READING: BOOK 6
The Queen Makes a Scene
Mairi Mackinnon
Illustrated by Mike and Carl Gordon
6